ALSO BY S.C. BARRUS

Novels

Discovering Aberration

The Gin Thief

Grim Curio - coming soon

Short Stories

Midway Between Heaven & Hell

The Hanging Gardens

THE PECULIAR CASE OF THE LUMINOUS EYE

S.C. BARRUS

AWAY & AWAY PUBLISHING

FOR TANA

1

The worms were ethereal blue, transparent, and began their disturbing existence by devouring the Subject's right eye. When first I saw them, I knew not whether they were biological or metaphysical, nor did I know how they came to be within the eye of the Subject. All I knew then was what the Housemaid had told me. She spoke of an eerie blue glow within a brown cavity in the Subject's eye and the way they twirled clockwise in a hypnotizing display.

IT WAS WELL into the evening and the rain pattered an irregular rhythm upon the cobbled streets. The Subject's housemaid, a dumpy old woman with a permanent blush of burst vessels in her cheeks, contacted me. She stood dripping, imploring me to make a house call and visit her employer who I shall refer to throughout as the Subject.

"He knows you're not a medical doctor, of course," she

said. She had nervous yet caring eyes though her complexion was poor.

I nodded. I was often mistaken for a medical practitioner. My work resided in a hazy area fluctuating between botany, biology, cryptology, and even—especially—the aether sciences.

"The Subject knows you by reputation," she continued, speaking his name, which I ignored quite deliberately. "He reads your reports and now he insists you are the only one he must see. None other, says he. In normal circumstances, I'd've said he's daft, but I've seen them, sir. It's a strange illness. Unnatural."

"Why is that, exactly?"

"The worms," she said with earnest appeal. "They are not of this world, sir. They glow blue and slither about his eye, causing pain like you wouldn't believe. I've never seen the Subject so much as admit to pain in my life. He may be thin and a recluse, but he's as strong a man as I've ever known. These strange worms are eating at him, sir, and he cannot bear it. He screams... Screams, clutching his eye, tries to pull the worms from it, but it cannot be done. Why, just hours ago he tasked me with the most frightening thing. He bade me pull these creatures from his eyeball, but my fingers slipped right through them. It could not be done. Oh, how he suffers!"

"Is that a fact?" My curiosity was fully piqued. "Glowing worms in the eye. That is most unusual. I have heard of worms that glow, but I've heard nothing of these parasites as you describe them. And you couldn't touch them, you say." My skin tingled uncomfortably. "It's been a while since anything made me shiver," I said with relish. "Right then. Please enter. I must hear more of this."

With a final fraught look back, she followed me into my office. The room was filled with artifacts collected from previous cases, which I retained partially as reference and partially as souvenirs to think back fondly on.

I sat at my desk, rearranged specimen jars filled with amber embalming fluids, and placed a notebook on the desk. The woman fidgeted as I took a quill from a skull of a three-eyed dog—a remnant of a previous investigation that now served as a quill holder.

"What are all these?" she asked nervously.

"Aren't they in excellent condition? So ripe, they appear to still be alive, don't they? I've become quite good at preserving my accomplishments, I must say. Look at this hand here, perfectly preserved. I found this hand crawling about, strangling unsuspecting victims. The act of a serial killer, the papers claimed, but no. It was our friend here. No need to look so frightened, my dearest. You are a client and I will take the utmost care of you. These jars are simply creatures unidentified by biological sciences. My work has me dealing with anomalies and conundrums of the strangest sort and, when my work is done, I collect the specimens, such as that strangling hand."

I interlaced my fingers. "Now, let us begin. We should not keep the Subject... ah, your employer, waiting long."

"His name is Mr—"

"No thank you. I don't do names of subjects. It triggers an empathetic part of my mind I find not conducive to my work. The Subject or employer will be fine."

"I... I see."

"Thanks. So, glowing worms in his eye, you said. And you attempted to remove them, unsuccessfully?"

"They are in his right eye," she replied. "Yes, attempted but I couldn't grasp them."

"Slippery? Or did they have too strong a hold on his eye and you feared damaging it?"

"Neither, sir. I couldn't touch the things. I pinched at them, but it was as if they passed through my tongs like ghosts. Could they be ghosts? I've heard frightful tales."

"Perhaps. Whatever the fact, they do sound like an interesting case. So rare a thing." I attempted to keep my mounting excitement concealed.

"There are several of them in his eye. At first, there was only one, and only a spot of blue at the time. We thought it a strange freckle, nothing more. But then it sprouted and more followed. Then the pain began, and when I looked again, I discovered a small pock in his eye. A hole. All this over the last few hours. Now several of the blue tails wriggle from the hole they've made. And when I left, the screaming, Heaven help him, it was horrible. We must be quick to return. He needs help."

I scrawled some notes as she spoke. She shuffled in her seat and glanced at the page.

I paused. "Sprouted from his eye, you said? It didn't plunge itself into it, but sprouted from it?"

"Yes. Like a weed. And then they began to twist."

"Very strange." I rubbed my chin as I thought on this decidedly un-wormlike trait. "Take me back to this morning when one of these worms, as you call them, sprouted from his eye. Had he been performing any new activities? Had he visited a sick friend, perhaps?"

"No." She shook her head. "He never leaves the house. Hasn't for years. Inherited a fortune and ever since stays holed up in the basement day and night, doing nothing but reading old books."

"Very curious," I mused, tapping my quill against my lip. "You might say he's a bookworm." I smiled, but the House-maid flinched at the innocent joke.

"Apologies," I said. I tasted ink, realized I'd smeared an inkblot on my lips again, and attempted to dab it clean with a handkerchief. "One develops an inappropriate sense of humor in my profession, I find. Anything else you can tell me?"

"No. I don't think so. Except. Perhaps there is one thing," she said, concentrating hard. "But surely this couldn't be related."

"Anything might be important."

"Well, he's always collected old books and his tastes have suddenly become quite macabre."

"What are these books about?"

"Not the subject, sir. The construction. Books bound in leather of... of humans, sir."

I choked in surprise. "Human?"

"Quite so. He told me all about them. He told me that some time back, books were often bound in human leather."

"Whatever for?"

"He said it was tradition for certain peoples of the world back in more savage days. A way to remember ancestors. It was an honor to be bound into a book, or so he told me. I have much distaste for the subject, so I didn't pay attention.

"Since he discovered this, he began sending out errand boys in search of these sorts of relics. They found nothing, of course. Apparently, few of these books survived the ages and most that did were burned upon discovery of what they were. I can't say I blame them."

"I see. So much for the memory of loved ones."

"Well, I suppose. But not long ago, maybe three weeks back, he hired an antiquities specialist. Paid him six months' wages and tasked him with searching the Earth for these sorts of books. Two nights ago, he received seven books, each bound in human skin. He went down to the basement to study them last night, and this morning returned complaining about the dust and a headache. Then the first worm sprouted from his eye."

2

The Subject had the quickness of breath, the tightness of muscle, and the twisted face of a man in agony. He was a lanky man with slicked-back hair and a long thin wispy beard—I wouldn't have suspected him rich had I not seen his opulent mansion or his ornate robe.

The mansion, with its long, unlit hallways and vaulted ceilings fading into darkness above us, put my studio to shame. For a moment, I cursed the rotten luck of working in a profession with inconsistent pay—such is the nature of anomalies: they happen so rarely.

Upon noticing our arrival, the Subject clasped a bottle of liquor in one hand, covered his right eye with the other, and shambled toward me with an irregular gait.

"Thank heavens you've come," he groaned. He tipped back the bottle and took a long drink. "It's all I can do to handle this." Timidly, he removed his hand from his eye and leaned close, wincing. "Is there any saving it? It's not normal. It's supernatural, isn't it? I've read your papers, I know the signs. I knew a doctor would miss something, so I called for you. Is there anything to be done? Please, for the love of all that's good, can I keep my eye?"

"There, there," I said. The emotions of others can put me quite on edge, but I pushed through the discomfort, placed a hand atop his head, and patted it. He flinched. "I'm here, and we will get to the bottom of your predicament soon enough. Housemaid, would you kindly lead the Subject to a chair? Perhaps the kitchen will do. Or any room without a rug. We don't want to stain any of these beautiful pieces, now do we? Was this rug imported? It is beautiful."

They gawked at me.

"Oh, come now." I looked from one to the other, suspecting I'd said something rude. "We must hurry. Chairs all around, if you please. And a bucket, perhaps, and some towels. Good heavens, look at that painting. That's an original, isn't it? You have a fine home. Don't just stand there. Chairs, chairs, chairs—spit spot."

"This way," said the Housemaid. She took the Subject by the arm and led him, groaning, through a ten-foot doorway into a hall with vaulted ceilings and exquisite tile floor. For all the elegance of the place, it was a bit drafty, so I buttoned up the collar of my jacket and rubbed my hands together as I wondered how much the Subject must pay for gas to run the furnace and all the lights.

All the way to the dining room the Subject groaned and hissed. "Heavens, it burns," he said again and again under his breath. The Housemaid led him to a chair at a massive table. It was a beautiful piece which I noticed was carved from a single piece of wood. Extraordinary, that such a tree may have existed anywhere in the world and was thence cut down, carved up, and ended up here, in this kitchen of all places. The small fortune this table must have cost astounded me.

This will do for a workshop, I thought. Perhaps the finest room I'd yet to work in, and about time too. *Heaven knows opportunities like this don't strike every day.* So I sat near the marvel and placed my magnification glasses on the tip of my nose.

"The lighting in here is—" I looked around, "—not quite adequate. Fetch us a lamp, Housemaid, if you'd be so kind. Now, sir, let's get a good look at those peepers, shall we? I've always wanted blue eyes. Alas, I was given brown and brown they shall remain."

With some hesitation, he removed his hand from his eye and watched me, mouth agape.

"Eyes," I said with a smile as I flipped first one magnifier and then another, until I could see the eerie blue twisting tails of these strange creatures in fine detail. "Eyes, eyes, eyes. I hate the feeling of getting so much as a lash in one of mine. I'll rub them raw, you know. It's only a lash but I'll itch and scratch until the irritation drives me looney. Can't imagine what it feels like to have these little fellers. They are marvelous, though, you have to admit."

As I studied the Subject, he focused on my face with his good eye, perhaps a mental trick to attempt to ignore the pain. "You're just as I imagined you'd be, you know," he said, voice shaking. "You make me feel worse and better. You can help me, can't you? I wasn't misguided in calling for you?"

"Too early to say," I said, absorbed in the ethereal blue tails spinning from the cavity in the black of his pupil. "They don't appear to be physical at all," I mumbled. "Your judgment on that account seems sound. But we may need to remove that eye, and I am not one for operations."

"Somehow... Somehow I'd thought you'd, I don't know, exorcize them... or something."

"Yes, yes, perhaps. If I knew more about them, that could be a possibility. All that is involved in an exorcism is finding the right deterrent. But we may not have time for that. No more questions now. I must work.

"No texture upon the blue," I said under my breath. "No skin nor membrane that I can see. They look like auras, with no real edges. They seem to fade away at high enough magnetism. Not ectoplasm, not defined enough for that.

"And they reside in the center of your eye, a pit. A pit. A small brown cavity. Interacting with physical material, eating away at it. No, these are not supernatural, as you might call it. No ghost worms—wouldn't that be a thing? It smarts, I shouldn't wonder. I have a cavity in my tooth and I can't stop tonguing it. Every time I do, I wince and hiss from the pain, but give it an hour and there I am doing it again. I never learn. But a cavity in the eye? Oh my, what an unusual thought."

I watched with amazement as the glowing protrusions twisted gently round and round. "Well, my friend. You know what I think? They are parasites, to be sure. And not exactly physical, as you surmised. I wonder if these worms are creatures at all, or some kind of shadow, a reflection of something else from another dimension. That would make sense. I have a feeling the real creatures are deeper still. In any case, I think you're in a spot of trouble."

"Trouble? Oh, fiery Hell. I can't... I can't take it. Just cut it out. Cut it out of me."

The Subject carried on thus for a moment or two, and I nodded and responded with, "Yes," and, "We shall see," and, "Indeed, quite so," while I pulled a rag and a bottle of ether from my bag, doused the rag in the liquid, then pressed it firmly over his nose and mouth. Oh, he struggled for a moment, but soon enough his eyes rolled back and his head thumped upon the table.

"What are you doing?" the Housemaid shrieked.

"Calm now," I said and tried to smile reassuringly. She stepped back. "We can't be premature about these things, you know. He'd be screaming for me to cut out his eye, and after a while, I'd give in and do it without all the information I need. I'm prone to suggestion, you see. So I have my own little tricks. Ether, for example. I can give you some if you think it'll help. I do indulge from time to time, and it takes the weight away. No? Well, that's fine. Perhaps you can remain quiet until I call on you, then. I have some thinking to do."

I n the following hours, I struggled to understand the nature of the strange anomaly. Wearing goggles and a mask, I pulled open the Subject's eye and watched those twisting things spin and cast their glow upon the white.

The ethereal parasites were like shadows, untouchable, yet they cast light and ate flesh. Not a usual combination. In my time I've witnessed untouchable creatures that devour consciousness. But the ethereal eating the physical... that is a rarer thing entirely.

Upon close examination, it appeared as though eye tissue was simply disappearing as if something were gobbling minuscule chunks, bit by bit. But matter cannot simply vanish. That I know of. I chewed on this for a while. Where was the by-product? The expulsion, waste, excrement, something cast off.

"Unless," I said as I watched the eye, "perhaps that's what you are after all?"

"Pardon?" said the Housemaid, jolted from her stupefied

daze. Beneath her eyes were purple bags, her hair hung limp, and her movement was becoming erratic. "Have you found something?"

"Perhaps," I said with little conviction. "Details. It's coming together, I think. I could be wrong. You have to open your eyes, in my line of work. Open them wide and let everything in. Without getting infected yourself, mind. That's just as important, if not more so. Absorb everything and your mind will piece it together eventually."

"And what detail have you noticed? Can you remove those disgusting things?"

I looked at her until she clasped her hands together nervously. "If I could, do you not think I would?" I said, palms on the cold table. "I am aware of the task at hand." I shook my head and turned back to the Subject. Then, after a moment, I sighed and said, "Apologies. On occasion I'm rude.

"In any case," I continued. "I don't think the threads are the problem. I'm starting to believe they are a symptom of something else. I've been rolling the word 'excretion' in my mouth for some time now. Could that be what we're seeing from his eye? Not worms, but other worldly excrement. Most foul, wouldn't you say?"

I spread my handkerchief upon the table and placed upon it scissors, forceps, tongs, scalpels, and of course, the gauze and antiseptic the use of any of these tools might require.

I first attempted to remove a worm with tongs but the metal slipped through. I experimented with a powerful magnet, which did nothing. Finally, I took a lever-action suction device from my bag, placed it over the man's eye, and pumped for all I was worth. When the pressure from the device was too high, I relieved it and tossed it aside where it fell to the floor with a clatter.

"Good thing for the ether, eh?" I said to the Housemaid. Her face was taut, every muscle engaged in pulling a horrified expression. This is it—that look I often see which signals my work has truly begun. "Could you imagine if I hadn't put him to sleep with the ether? This whole process would be unbearable. So much noise and struggle. No, it's better this way. This way I can concentrate."

All the while, the dreadful cavity in the Subject's eye expanded piece by minuscule piece.

"It seems we've reached a conundrum," I told the Housemaid as I scratched my scalp with fingers moist with sweat. I glared at the eye through my magnifying lens. There was nothing I could identify but the glow, even with exploratory incisions. "Blast, I thought I'd find something. I don't feel comfortable pushing forward with him at this point. I know anomalies, but anatomy is... I need a doctor. The cavity is getting deeper. Housemaid, you will make another call, won't you?"

"I can do anything, sir," she said in a weary voice, the edges of her mouth twitching.

"We'll need a proper doctor. That eye must be popped right out and I, sadly, am not the one for that job. Here, hurry to this address and fetch the doctor there, a Dr. Florence. Tell her it is I who sent for her and that it's urgent. She may attempt to turn you away. If she does, give her this envelope and tell her there's more. She'll come."

"What is it?"

"We all have our vices, don't we? While you're fetching her, I'll poke around the Subject's new book collection. Perhaps we'll discover something in there. Pray the cavity gets no deeper in the meantime. Removing his brain shan't be as simple as removing his eye."

4

I sat on the table and watched the Subject. I couldn't help but wonder at this man's life, at the things his dying eye had seen before the worms, or whatever they may be, ate at it. Horrific things, I theorized. A man this wealthy, with tastes as macabre as his... If I were to poke around, I was sure to uncover a corpse or two in the closet, so to speak.

Oh, this man had seen things, all right. Like me. I suspect one morning I'll wake and find a worm or two in my eye. If not a worm, some other parasite, a haunting or foul thing. No doubt. No doubt about that at all.

"What a table," I said aloud, as I ran my finger along it and watched the fitfully slumbering man. Not only was the magnificent table cut from a single piece of wood, but the pattern of the grain was breathtaking, and the richness in color—deep browns highlighted by wine-red rivulets—was sublime.

"I wonder if I could fit this in my studio. Ha! Who am I kidding? Maybe a quarter of it split down the middle and across... If I get rid of my desk, that could work. And I'd have to move the bookshelf, I think. Strain my back in the process."

I was starting to feel glum as I watched the spinning blue threads and the ever-growing cavity. From this distance, they seemed to wriggle rather than twist.

"If I save for long enough, I might be able to purchase a table such as this. Heavens, what could it be worth? A few thousand? It won't ever happen. Don't fool yourself."

I grabbed at my hair, shook my head in an attempt to turn my attitude around. "It will happen, it will happen, I just have to keep moving forward, keep taking advantage of... of situations laid out before me. Situations like this one." I perked up. "Oh. Oooooh. This one. This could change my life if I play it right. Good heavens. This could be the one that pushes me into legitimacy. Blast it! I hadn't thought of that. And I never brought up my fee. I need something, need it in writing or this whole opportunity might slip through my fingers."

The Subject's left eyelid twitched. His right eye glowed bright. With a grimace, the Subject gasped and, in a flash, sat up straight, howling, clasping at his face.

"Please!" He looked at me with his hollow blue eye. "Please, the pain!"

I hopped down from the table and stood over him with my hands in my jacket pockets. It was cold in here. Too cold. "I can help with the pain." I patted my satchel. "A dab more ether will lessen it considerably."

"Yes!" he cried. "Please."

"And I will attempt to save your life as best I can. But, my dearest Subject, I need some assurances. You understand." I pulled from my satchel a notebook, ink, and quill, then jotted down a few lines, ignoring the man's confused protests. "Here," I said. "I want you to sign this. Standard contract. We were in such a hurry when I arrived, I nearly forgot to have you sign it."

"Contracts?" cried the man. "Contracts? My eye!"

"Yes, it is unfortunate that without a contract I cannot continue to work. I need protection, and I have very little but pen and ink to do so, you understand. I am writing that, regardless of outcome, I am to be owed fifteen thousand. And a bonus upon a positive outcome, whatever that may be. The costs of ocular anomalies, I'm afraid. Do please sign."

"Damn it!" he cried, his face a quivering mask. "I've... made arrangements. I'm offering you my house, the top floor, as a... workshop. Should I die, you retain the deed. Now give me that damn ether."

"I don't suppose..." I hesitated, then sighed. "I don't suppose you have that in writing somewhere I can see it?"

"Piece of shit. The lobby, on a small table by the closet. Now give me the bleeding ether!"

I considered whether to investigate, but that seemed rude at this particular point in time. I had an inkling that I hadn't come across in the manner I had hoped, but it was too late to make amends now. Maybe I am a piece of shit, I don't know. Or maybe I'm just trying to survive in a harsh world. Could be both.

"Why thank you," I said. "I do appreciate a patron. Truly." A tear welled up in my eye. What was I feeling? Perhaps happiness or something like it. I thought about working in a building like this one. Perhaps I was finally making it. Hard work and persistence over time is sure to add up to something.

I dabbed the cloth in ether and sent him back into fitful sleep.

5

The Subject stored his collection in the mansion's basement. There I descended in search of human-skin bound books. The basement was cold, dark, and massive. Without the assistance of the Housemaid, I was unable to find the lever to fire the gas lamps, so I searched by the light of my lantern. It cast a small orange glow, elongated shadows, and dimly lit rows of shelfs, book piles, trash heaps, and hoarded things.

Piles upon piles of books were heaped in all corners and stacked precariously along the walls. They were formed into makeshift tables which in turn were covered in newspapers, dirty glasses, and bottles with cobwebs sprouting from their necks to the books they rested upon. Boxes and crates and chests—some open, others nailed shut—filled every cranny.

"Lifestyle of the rich and neurotic," I muttered as I searched the dark maze of junk.

Following a makeshift path, I discovered the unique collection of books I sought collected within a chest and stacked atop one another like any other benign thing. I ran a finger over one. The skin was cold and clammy.

"Seven books bound in flesh," I mused. "How does one inquire about these, I wonder? 'Excuse me, bookseller, you don't happen to have a book made from genuine people do you? It would please me ever so much to find one. Would you be a dear and look in the back? I have to say, I've been searching for a book made from a person for quite some time and nobody's been willing to assist me.'"

The topmost book had a strange nub at the corner of the cover—a nipple. I wondered if they shaved the dead before stripping their skin, or would I find a book with a sprouting of armpit hair on the back? I chuckled at the thought. The sound echoed eerily and sent a shiver down my spine.

Once again I donned my goggles, gloves, and a respiratory mask, then performed a cursory examination of the books for any signs of the worm-like creatures. Finding none, I took a breath, reached out tentatively, and moved the nearest book with a fingertip. The hair on my arms stood stiff and I found myself quite on edge.

But there was nothing out of sorts other than a nipple here, a dimple or a freckle there. Simply books in various states of decay. The topmost book seemed to be excellently preserved but the others had not aged so well. The bindings were frail, the pages brittle, and as I cautiously flipped through them, I found no sign of any nefarious creature, no ghostly spawn, nor other creepish imaginings.

I grumbled to myself, a little disappointed. I placed the books back within their chest in two stacks, then contemplated them for a long while. And then it struck me. The Housemaid had said there were seven books here, but no, the piles were even. I counted and found six. I looked around in the dim light.

A call came from the stairway.

"Sir!" A light twinkled in the distance, indicating that the Housemaid had returned. "I've brought Dr. Florence, sir. Come quick, the Subject seems to have taken a turn!"

"Coming," I shouted back and my words echoed in the great chamber. I moved to step away when the heel of my boot slipped upon a slick surface and I tumbled to the floor. "Damn it!" I shouted. "You'd think a man who could pay for all this could afford to keep the damn place tidy. Where does that Housemaid do her housemaiding?"

But then I paused. There was something in the air, some-thing very subtle, a dusty haze drifting in the darkness that I hadn't noticed before. I lit a match and held it aloft, watched the individual specks of haze rise and dissipate. I extin-guished the flame, then grabbed the lamp from the corner of the chest to better illuminate the room. The light caught the haze just as the last of it dissipated.

"Sir," came the call again, "Please, hurry."

I ignored the Housemaid and examined what I had tripped over. Another book, but this one was coated in a film like mucus or mold. There were fingerprints upon it too. The Subject's, no doubt. And evidence of a skid on the cover—ah, my heel where I slipped. I probed the mucus with the dead match and another puff of dust spat into the air, then dissipated.

"That is interesting," I thought, looking the mucous over, holding my breath as I neared it, though I still wore the mask. A thought struck me. I reached within my satchel and pulled out a piece of deep blue resin and broke off a chunk, then placed the resin within the lamp. The flame sputtered, then began to cast a violet glow. And the film upon the book lit, sparkling with intensity.

"That mucus is not of this world," I whispered. "My, my. You may be the culprit, then."

6

I returned to the dining room, having left the book behind which I wrapped in canvas for quick retrieval. Upon entering, I found Dr. Florence wearing an overcoat with the white of a nightgown peeking out at her ankles. Her black hair was a mess, strands of it puffing out at all angles, yet the sight of her still made my heart thump. *Don't say anything stupid*, I thought. *Our last encounter was a disaster. This is the only second chance you'll ever get.*

She hunched over the Subject, tapping the rim of her spectacles with a look of incredulity—tiny thoughtful wrinkles around the ridge of her nose—which I found so appealing. Perhaps she was pale, with a basement tan like mine, but that only made the black of her eyebrows all the more intense, like an illustration or text on a snake oil label.

"There you are, Willem. You know, I didn't believe it," she said without looking up. My breath caught in my throat at the sound of my name. Hearing it from her was lovely and nerve-wracking. "I thought this another farce. I told the Housemaid that I'd wring both of your necks if it were a charade. Did I not?"

"She did, sir," said the Housemaid. "But I assured her, and now she's here."

Dr. Florence looked at me over her round spectacles for a long moment. I swallowed. There was a smidge of white powder under her nose. She had taken my gift and, clearly, she was not happy about it.

"Well, luckily for us all, his eye is properly mangled," I said with a nervous smile. They both looked at me strangely, but I continued. "My cases have never once been a farce. Not on my end, anyway. But I can forgive your accusations. Perhaps this matter can return us to an even footing. In any case, you've seen the eye. What do you make of it?"

"It's distressing," she said. Yes, it was distressing. The cavity had grown, the blue threads were longer and more numerous, though they spun slow and haunting the same as ever. "I've never seen anything quite like it," she said. She watched the spinning threads, hypnotized.

"Nor I," I replied. It was hard to look away from them, despite the rotten and ever-expanding cavity that caused my skin to prick at the sight of it. "It's an unusual case, I should think. The eye is turning rotten. Normally I'd continue gathering information or attempting to exorcize them, but I fear that's no longer the most prudent course of action. Hence your invitation."

"It's foul." She grimaced, though her eyes held a twinkle of macabre fascination. I do so enjoy the company of people who take pleasure in their craft, and the fact that she was somewhat perturbed with me made it all the more enjoyable, though I cannot say why.

"They," she said, "whatever they are, those blue strings, they've eaten through his eye. You should have called me earlier—we could have removed it before they reached anything vital. But now... Now I'm not so sure. I'll need to poke around during the operation to know for certain."

Dr. Florence placed her mobile medicine cabinet upon the kitchen table and drew the doors open to display a collection of medicines, compartments with cloth and scalpels, and a small shelf labeled 'Poison, do not ingest'. "What are your thoughts on these creatures, Willem?"

My thoughts, indeed. I was still formulating my opinion, but pieces seemed to be falling in place. "It is a conundrum. They don't appear to be physical at all. As slippery as shadows. They respond to neither suction nor magnetism. Instruments seem to pass right through them, clean as can be. And look closely, Doctor, do they not seem to be translucent? No skin to speak of.

"But creature? I do believe these are not worms at all, as the Housemaid and the Subject have claimed, but perhaps evidence of some deeper unseen source, something else, glowing ethereal shadows. From what I gather, this is more like an otherworldly fungus, or something along those lines. That's my current theory, in any case."

"Will it be safe to remove his eye?" asked the Housemaid with concern.

"Safe?" Dr. Florence spat. "We are well past safe. Help me strap him to the table."

I smiled at the request, tried to think of something coy to say, then bit my tongue. Instead, I said, "And such a nice table it is, wouldn't you say? Cut from a single tree, I believe."

"Pardon?" she replied then shook her head and frowned. "Help me lift, will you."

The doctor, housemaid, and I set the rigid man upon the table, pulled tight his stiff limbs, and strapped him down.

"This is very advanced," Dr. Florence said. "Removing the eye will lessen the chance of infection and hopefully remove this fungus, or whatever it is, in the process. But beyond this, I fear there may not be much more I can do for him. Strange creatures, aren't they?"

She sniffed, rubbed her nose, then cracked her knuckles one by one. "My better judgment says we must quarantine him, that we too must be quarantined lest the worst happen and we spread the parasite. After we operate, none of us can leave this house until we are sure we have not been infected."

7

It was a pleasure to watch Dr. Florence at work. I'd seen her work before, performing an amputation. At that time, her deftness of skill, the way she set her jaw as she lowered the bonesaw, the way wisps of black hair fell over her face and she blew them away, huffing, sweating, sawing back and forth, all seemed magical. I'd endeavored to work with her again ever since, and thus discovered her proclivity to... Well, a gentleman keeps a lady's secrets.

She pinned her hair back with a surgical clamp, and rolled up the sleeves to her black overcoat, exposing the white lace of her nightgown. Then she took forceps and scalpel in hand, and delved into the Subject's face with such precision and mastery, I could not help but be impressed once again. Nary a drop of blood speckled her porcelain skin from the moment of incision until she plopped out the eyeball, trimmed the viscera, and held it aloft like a trinket.

"Exemplary job," I said. "Exemplary."

"Thank you." She wiped the sweat from her forehead with her overcoat sleeve. "They seem to have remained in the eye, see." She turned the cavity toward me, and the strange blue threads continued to spin.

She set the eyeball within a pool of alcohol I'd poured upon a plate. I took a match and set it alight. The eye burned and spat and sputtered. The twisting blue threads slowed, faded, disintegrated, and—finally—vanished entirely.

I took out a handkerchief and offered it to Dr. Florence.

"Thank you," she said again and dabbed her forehead.

"I get chills watching you work," I said. "Like watching a splendid performance in the theater when chills creep along your spine. Do you know what I mean?"

"It's called a frisson. Yes, I know what you mean, though I never get such chills. Not everybody does."

"Oh," I said, a little disappointed. I slipped on gloves, located a small jar, and with all the alcohol burned away, brushed the remains within it. "Well," I said, "thanks for the fine work, regardless."

The Housemaid, watching the jar with a frown, piped up. "What are you planning to do with his eye?"

"I will need to study it." I smiled and tilted my head. "So much to learn, you know. And it's non-negotiable. Part of my fee."

Dr. Florence gathered gauze and wrapping.

"Did you see anything in there?" I asked as she dressed the area. "Any other signs?"

"Another cavity," she said. "Just at the base of the socket. I saw none of these worms, none of that strange light. My hope is that the problematic tissue has been removed. But we should certainly be cautious, as I have said, and quarantine ourselves for the gestation period. Two days, I should think. But as for signs of this disease spreading, nothing of note."

"Mind if I take a look before you close up the socket?"

"Be my guest."

I donned my magnification glasses and peered within the empty red space. "Cleanly done," I said.

"Yes, you mentioned. Frisson-inducing."

I scanned the cavity and searched for any possible evidence of further infection. "A little sign around the eye cavity, but that's to be expected. In my experience, a residue is common. Otherwise, they, the wormy things, appear to be gone. That doesn't mean we're in the clear, as you said. My methods of detecting etheric residues are elementary at best. Time will tell."

Dr. Florence didn't respond. Instead, she set to work disinfecting her instruments and cleaning her workspace.

"We do what we can with what tools we have, I suppose," I said, trailing off. Then something caught my attention. "Wait a moment. What's this?" Was it my imagination, or was there something clinging to the edge of the cavity? I increased magnification by flipping another lens over my glasses and peered diligently.

"When one removes an eye, what tends to be left behind?" I asked. "Should there be a... hmm..."

"What?"

"There seems to be a film. I can barely make it out, but come, look at this. Is that normal?"

She leaned close, looked at the socket, moved her head back and forth. "I don't see... Oh, yes. There is something... very faint. Almost translucent." She took my lenses from me and peered closer. "Yes. I didn't notice it earlier but..."

"Housemaid," I said. "Would you kindly find a clump of resin from within my satchel."

"Of course," she said and rummaged through it. Her back went rigid and she looked to me for a moment before announcing, "Why sir, you have a flintlock in here. Whatever for?"

"Tool of the trade," I replied. "The resin, please. Not that one. Ah, there you have it. Yes, that's the one. Now turn out the lamps in the room again, all but one, and place the resin in it."

She did as instructed and the lamp glowed violet. As I feared, within the Subject's eye socket was a dab of film, surrounding the tiny cavity, which glowed the faintest blue.

"What does that mean?"

"Ethereal," I said. "Let us hope removing the eye causes it to fade away. Otherwise, we may need to operate further."

8

There was nothing further to be done but quarantine ourselves and wait. We three were confined to a sitting room where the constant ticking of a massive upright clock provided a measure of the quarantine, its tocks giving every second a lingering feeling, as if time had slowed merely due to us being so aware of it.

We placed the Subject in a separate room with an open door that allowed constant observation. Next to his sleeping body, I placed a bottle of brandy, some ether, and a cloth for him to administer the drug to himself should he wake in a bout of pain.

"In the morning we'll undergo another thorough examination," stated Dr. Florence as we settled in our various spaces. "If there are no symptoms or signs, I would say we are safe to return to our daily lives."

As night progressed, the Housemaid stared off at nothing in particular, rocking and humming until she lay on the floor and drifted to sleep. Dr. Florence took to a chair and, after a time, nonchalantly dipped her finger within the envelope I'd gifted her. It came out white and she sucked away the residue, then licked her teeth. I looked away when she caught my eye.

"How did you know?" she asked plainly.

I hesitated. I knew this moment would come, yet I hadn't determined what to say. So I shrugged and avoided her eyes. "We all have our vices," I replied. "I tend to keep track."

"You keep track? You're a little disturbed, aren't you?"

"I don't think so." This wasn't the thread I hoped she'd follow. "Though you wouldn't be the first to accuse me thus."

"And what is yours, then? Your vice?"

"Well, I'm an ass," I said with a testing smile. I glanced at her but the smile wasn't returned. She worked her jaw while she watched me without any sign of emotion. "So I've been told."

"Yes. Come now," she said. "Is that all you'll share with me? We have the entire night to while away. I'll extract the truth from you one way or another. May as well keep things cordial and tell me. Give me a more interesting vice. Tit for tat."

I scratched my neck. "Isn't it cold in here?" I pulled a shawl from a nearby shelf and wrapped myself in it.

"You're stalling."

"I don't think you'll like it."

"You've killed people?" she asked abruptly. "Haven't you? You murder people in their sleep."

I couldn't tell if she was being serious or if this was her odd sense of humor surfacing. I watched her and she gave no sign, so I asked, "Is that what you think of me?"

She smiled wryly before her expression faded again. "No,

but I wouldn't be surprised if it were true. Come on then, out with it."

I wondered, even as I formed the words, whether I should tell the truth. "Sometimes I—oh, how to put it?—I follow people."

"Follow people? For work? Like a detective?"

"Yes," I said, perking up. "Just like a detective. Except, well, it's not always entirely professional."

"You're a stalker?"

"Ah," I laughed nervously. I picked up a pillow from the floor—red fabric with a swirling pattern of smooth and dull textures—and I stared at it and nodded. "I suppose you could call it that."

"I should have known."

"It's all innocent." I fingered the tassels on the pillow's edge, ran my fingers through them again and again until they were tangled. "I never threaten anyone, I wish no one harm, I'm just... curious about how certain people spend their days."

"And you followed me?"

I didn't reply, so she craned her neck until I couldn't help but meet her eyes. She raised an eyebrow.

"Yes," I said, feeling the weight of guilt. "Only for a little."

"I see. And did you see anything untoward?"

"Not especially." I'd seen glimpses of her from my place in the hedgerow. I watched her reading in her nightgown. I watched her brew tea and stretch her neck and stare long-ingly out into the darkness. I watched her sit motionless in her loneliness, then sniff some drug and hurry about tidying the house. Later, she drank a few glasses of wine and fell asleep on her chair. I watched her sleep for a time, let exhaustion overtake me, fought it and continued watching, my head supported by leaves until I could hardly keep my eyes open. Then I walked home cloaked in the knowledge that she was as lonely as I, and though she did not know it, we were together in our loneliness. "I never saw anything... untoward, as you say."

"Liar. I don't... know how I feel about this." She eyed me, tapping her finger against the rim of her glasses while she worked her jaw.

I looked up from my pillow, glanced away when I met her eyes, then looked again. I asked, "What are you thinking?"

"I'm figuring out how I feel about you."

"Oh," I said, and swallowed. "Take your time."

"I intend to. I've never been followed before. Did you peer through my windows?"

"I don't know what to say. Yes. A little."

She shivered. "That's frightening." Though she didn't sound frightened. I wanted to look inside her brain, to know what she was thinking. "And what of my curtains?"

"They are very sheer. I'd thought—"

"You thought what?"

"I thought maybe you chose sheer curtains because a part of you wanted someone to look inside." Saying this aloud made me realize how stupid a thought it had been.

There was that flash of a smile again, disappearing before I could even be sure I saw it. Was I not wrong? Had she been daydreaming of one such as I spying on her mundane activities?

"And that's how you discovered my vice?"

"Yes."

"Well," she said dryly, looking at me over the brim of her

glasses. "That's not fair. I must discover yours myself, then. I'm not interested in hearing any more of this stalking nonsense. I don't think I'll believe it lest I see it for myself. I'll keep an eye out, and if I discover I have something to fear, I shall alert you."

I hesitated as I decoded her words. Was she asking me to continue? "You'll keep an eye out?" My throat felt thick.

There was the slightest twitch at the edge of her lips. "Yes. Two eyes if I can spare them. Now, I'll hear no more of it. You should get some sleep. You seem positively beside yourself, Willem."

My cheeks flushed. In the door to this room was a small window. I peered out to check on the Subject, who slept with shuddering breaths. "I shan't be sleeping tonight. I'll keep my eyes on our subject until this affair is over. Should anything happen, I'll need to be quick to respond." I yawned, then shook my head.

Dr. Florence looked down at her small envelope, then extended it to me. "It'll keep you awake," she said. "It helps me toil away for endless hours."

I dabbed a finger. "You did a magnificent job with that eye, by the by. Incredible. I would've botched the whole thing."

9

It was near four in the morning when I was ripped from my stupor by a creak from a floorboard in the hall. I rose from my place, saw the Housemaid and Dr. Florence both soundly sleeping. I turned to look into the hall, then gasped when I saw him there as the door swung open.

The Subject grabbed at the doorframe, clawing at it, attempting to support himself, knees buckling. His one good eye searched, blinking, pulling strings of mucus across it with sticky smacking sounds. He moaned and coughed and hacked and wheezed. Arm outstretched, he shambled haphazardly, step by shaking step. His good eye rolled about strangely and his empty socket was coated in a thick white film.

The film burnt an afterimage of red and blue in my vision, so even when I blinked its ethereal display seared my mind, nearly stunning me.

The Subject opened his mouth and sounds came forth, muffled and damp. I could see the disgusting film inside his mouth, dense as cotton, and when his lips closed the vision of an open maw burnt a red and blue image of a howling specter into the backs of my retinas.

I broke myself out of the spell, saw the others shaken awake. Their tired eyes gawked at the Subject for a moment before turning away from the searing vision of color. I grabbed my respirator and pulled it into place as I shouted, "Masks on, quickly does it."

Dr. Florence shivered, shook her head and blinked rapidly, then shouted in alarm as the Subject stumbled to the center of the room. She wrapped her cloth mask about her face and rose from her chair.

He stood between the three of us, his knees buckled, then his entire body crumpled. He fell hard to the floor, splayed out. After a moment of silence, his neck twisted around with loud popping noises until his face was directly above his back. His damp, mold-covered mouth opened and closed, issuing desperate rasps.

My own breath rushed through my respirator as I wiped sweat from my brow and stepped nearer. I reached a hesitant hand toward him. He looked more dead than alive—his iris a milky gray. Just then, his body trembled, hands quivered violently, arms and legs spasmed. Clotted gray mucus frothed from his mouth.

"He can't be alive," Dr. Florence said, voice somehow still steady—only the speed of her speech gave away any hint of nerves. "We must leave the room now." She pressed her mask tight against her face. "There's no saving him."

The Subject shook more violently. Froth and film and grit were flung in clumps from side to side. We both jumped back and moved quickly toward the door.

But the Housemaid dashed toward him, called out his

name and begged, "You're alright, you're alright," as if saying the words somehow made the sentiment real. "He'll be fine," she said, blinking wildly, inching closer while leaning away from the spew. "Help him."

In no time at all, the Subject's muscles seized, and his entire body tensed as if it would curl in on itself. A long, boggy exhalation, an eruption of ash and snotty viscera, exploded from him.

"Close the do—"

The Subject's death rattle transformed into an impossible, throatless bellow. My very bones quaked at the wretched sound of it. When I blinked, red and blue flashes of a writhing specter seared my mind's eye.

With that unnatural endless exhalation, he spewed a pillar of thick, foaming dust into the air with such force I thought his head would burst. The Housemaid's face was enveloped in it, surrounded by the spew of dust and grime as it ripped past her and struck the ceiling where it bloomed about the room.

Dr. Florence and I slammed the door shut and leaned upon it panting, watching through the window as the contents of the room disappeared in the cloud.

Over the haunting bellow and the sounds of scrambling, crying, and the screams of the Housemaid, Dr. Florence yelled, "There's no hope for her now. She's infected."

"And there'll be none for us if we don't seal this door," I replied, lifting the mask to my forehead.

The view through the window was darkened by a fog so thick I could not see more than inches within the room, yet still I saw the ghostly flashes of writhing on the backs of my eyes.

"Do you see it?" I shouted.

Dr. Florence, shielding her face, shouted, "Yes."

From within the impossibly thick cloud appeared the Housemaid. She struck against the door, screaming and clawing. Black tears ran down her cheeks. "Please," she wailed, her voice muffled by the murky substance within her throat. "Please."

Dr. Florence and I looked at each other and made a silent resolution not to acknowledge the doomed woman.

"Quick," I shouted. "What can we seal the door with?"

"There are blankets in all these rooms—I'll grab one and wet it. That should work for a time."

"Yes!" I shouted. "There are hammer and nails in my case on the table—grab that too. Quickly now."

"Please!" cried the Housemaid. "I didn't know."

Dr. Florence ran down the hall and disappeared around the corner.

Our faces separated only by a layer of glass, I watched the Housemaid as her eyes slowly sprouted nubs of vivid blue, first one then another until, within moments, hundreds grew and glowed, all of them twisting. I held the door shut and shouted, "Where are you?"

"I'm coming," Dr. Florence shouted back as she rounded the corner. She tossed a pile of sopping wet blankets at my feet, then pulled from her wet jacket a hammer and nails.

She ran into the next room. I heard a long squealing sound, and when I looked back I saw her pulling a large chair. "To blockade the door." She pulled it to me, and as the Housemaid thudded against the door again and again, we positioned the chair into place.

Then the Housemaid stopped.

All was quiet. Through the window I saw only gray stillness. Even the fog seemed to clot and solidify.

"Do you suppose..." I trailed off.

"She must be—"

The glass shattered. As shards fell around us, I closed my eyes and jumped away. A fist, sliced along the wrists and oozing blood, hung limply from the window. Coagulated smoke, clotted and putrescent, oozed from the window in gross configurations. The hand opened, grabbed at the air, slapped against the door leaving a bloody print, then grabbed the jagged glass to pull the short woman up even as it sliced her through. Her face appeared amid the shattered glass, haloed by thousands of spinning blue threads.

"Step back," shouted Dr. Florence. She pulled my flintlock from her jacket, having apparently grabbed it when she took the hammer from my satchel. She held it inexpertly before her, tilted her head as she took aim at the bleeding, glowing, gnashing woman, closed her eyes tight, and fired.

The Housemaid's head flipped back. Like cotton ripped apart, the frozen fog tore and then swallowed her up. As it tore it released a small amount of haze, a dusting like I'd seen when I prodded the book in the basement.

"Shit," muttered Dr. Florence as she stepped back, blinking hard. She tossed the flintlock to the ground, turned quickly, and hurried back down the hall.

"Where are you going?" I called, then followed after her, leaving behind the strange carnage.

"Shit!" she shouted. "Damn it!"

I paused. That puff of dust, did it get to her? She had avoided the violent spew, but then that last little dusting...

"How are you?" I asked when I caught up to her.

"Fan-bloody-tastic," she said, and for the first time, her voice no longer hid her emotion. "Why? How are you feeling?" She swore and flung her wet jacket to the floor, grabbed at her nightgown, and rubbed her eye raw. "Damn it!" she shouted, clenching her fists. She stormed toward the stairway.

"Where are you going?"

"To the kitchen."

It had got her. No denying that. "It's in your eye."

She ignored me, slammed a wall with her palm, then descended the stairway, taking the steps two at a time.

It had got her, alright, but not as badly as the Housemaid. No, more like when the Subject first caught this disturbing disease from the book.

"Where are your supplies?" I asked. "Back in the room?"

"I don't know," she said, midway down the stairs. "No. On the table."

I knew how this would end: with me cutting. My stomach turned queasy and I tensed at the thought as I watched her descend. I grimaced and hurried after her, through the dining room, past the table with our instruments and binding-twine still arranged upon it, and shouted, "What are you doing?"

I heard a splash of water from the kitchen. When I entered, her head was submerged in a bucket of water. She remained thus for half a minute before she came out, gasping for air.

"What are you doing?" I shouted again.

She rose abruptly. Water drenched her hair and ran down her nightgown as she marched to a cabinet, throwing open the doors. I saw her right eye and it was red.

"Hey!" I shouted. She was acting mad. I watched as she flung open one cabinet and then another, each one more violently than the last. She yanked open the fourth so hard that it rebounded and slammed shut again.

"Shit! Damn it!"

"It's your eye, isn't it?"

She folded her arms and focused on the floor, then nodded. She marched back to the bucket, falling to her hands and knees, but I grabbed her arm and shouted, "Talk to me! I can help."

"I'm flushing out my eye."

She was soaking, shivering, distressed. I tried to meet her eyes, but she looked away. I moved until she could not but look at me.

"Let me see," I said.

Her hands quaked. Left eye clear, right eye irritated. "It stings," she said.

"Yes. I imagine it does." I couldn't tell if she was shivering from fright or from the cold and the wet, so I removed my jacket and wrapped it about her shoulders. "But here's the good news. Your symptoms aren't as acute as the House-maid's. The effects are progressing at a slower rate, like the Subject. That means we have some time. But we were unable to—"

She broke away from me, opened the cabinet and found a bottle of liquor, uncorked it, and tipped it back. She drank in great gulps, then leveled her eyes on me, one white, the other cherry red, and said, "We need to cut it out."

She was right. And I'd be the one doing the cutting. I held my breath. Why did I have to be the person to cut her so? Could I even do it? Not as well as she, certainly. But I'd try.

Because, in the end, whether for good or ill, I was my profession, and I would do everything I could to resolve this anomaly with as few victims as possible. If that meant that one should die in order to prevent an outbreak, so be it. If that meant destroying my chance at a relationship with the woman I'd been pining for, fine. I'd do the cutting. Things always have a way of getting messy when I work—I'd hoped to avoid it, but such is life.

"Yes," I said, sadly. "I will need to cut it out before it advances."

"Let's prepare the table," she said. Her body shook but her voice had become even as she slipped back into her persona of a medical professional. It was a thin veil—clearly, she was frightened—but it protected her all the same. "I'll talk you through the process before we begin—"

A thump sounded from the floor above. I tensed, looked at the ceiling, held my breath, and listened. For a time, nothing. Then, as I exhaled slowly, another bump sounded. "Of all the—"

Through the ceiling came a muffled retching sound, another bang, then a crash.

"She's alive?" I whispered.

"Or the parasite has taken over," Dr. Florence said. "Like your Subject before her, she's dead, but the thing within her has control now. Willem, she cannot leave this house. We must burn it down."

I nodded.

"Willem," she said again, nearing me. Then she kissed me hard on the lips. I froze in shock. I blinked and shook my head, tried to reason what had just happened as she stepped back and looked away. "We cannot risk an outbreak."

But her words were now but a hum. In my mind's eye, I stepped toward her and kissed her back passionately, but here I was attempting to find my senses and return to the scene at hand. Outbreak?

I swallowed and managed to breathe. "Can't risk it."

"Not from her, not from either of us. I'll prepare the table. See to her quickly. Worst comes to the worst, we'll burn this place down with us inside." She winced and cupped her hand over her eye. "Ahh. Willem, it's starting, I can feel it."

"Gather your instruments." My faculties returned as I moved to leave. "Best as you can. I'll start the fire."

10

I set my jaw and pulled my mask and goggles into position. I could hear the Housemaid clawing at the floor. I ran to the stairs, where I was met by echoing gags and disconcerting popping sounds. Somehow she sounded larger and utterly inhuman. The walls and ceiling were already splotched with white fuzz, which made the tiny mask I wore seem frightfully inadequate.

Nothing tethered me to this house—I could have run, locked the doors from the outside, and let the infected, including the Doctor, burn. It was the smart thing to do, careful and thorough. I played with this idea like a hard candy, but when I looked back into the dining room and saw Dr. Florence tipping back alcohol with one hand and preparing for operation with the other, I couldn't leave her to burn. It wasn't a matter of morals, it was infatuation.

I walked up the stairs slowly, the hairs on the back of my neck standing on end. I hadn't decided what I'd do, driven by impulse, by the need to gather more information. The higher

I climbed, the more noises reached me—now accompanied by crunching wood, the sounds of something dragging—causing me to flinch and test each step.

When the hall came into view, I beheld drapes of white mold thicker than an infestation of spider webs. I blinked and my vision was seared with red and blue after-images so intense that I gasped in shock. I had to strain to see, and when I blinked again it was like getting punched in the face with the intensity of the vision. I held my eyes open, forced myself not to blink and to let the searing images fade, and took in the view—so white and rotten, it looked as though the walls were ready to crumble and topple down.

My breath caught in my throat. A contorted black appendage—an oozing, elongated arm—clawed at the air, the Housemaid's body hanging from it. The thing emerged like a network of putrescent veins from her, from the very cuts. The appendage hit the moldy back wall, which shook and crunched. Thin tendrils like antennae probed the mold. They jittered, took root in the wall. The limb jolted as it pulled behind it the wretched body of the Housemaid, her mouth agape, rasping and drooling gray muck.

The Housemaid was crowned in a halo of glowing blue so thick, twisting, and unnerving. She gripped at the floor and walls, pulled herself forward slowly, wailed silently, and spewed chunks of coagulated gray.

One blink was all it took to shock me back to life and drive me to nausea. I turned and ran back down the stairs, then hurried to the dining room where Dr. Florence waited, scalpel in hand like a weapon.

"What's going on out there?"

What was going on? Our sweet Housemaid, shot and left for dead, and the thing inside her had seemingly mutated and now cursed this house to fester and rot. But I could only think to say, "Grab a chair. She is coming."

"A chair?"

"Yes!"

I grabbed a chair in each hand, took up my lamp awkwardly, and shuffled out of the room. "Hurry," I shouted back. I could barely see the top of the stairs for the banister, but as I neared, long and thin black tendrils came into view above me, testing the air and flicking about. When I reached the foot of the stairs, I could see her—or rather, that convulsing parasite that used to be the Housemaid—spewing gray smoke that rolled up the walls and then slowed, atrophied so stiff that it hung in the air like pillars of cotton.

I tossed my chairs onto the stairs, then turned to find Dr. Florence behind me carrying more.

"Make a barricade," I said, and she tossed hers also. The stairway was wide, our pathetic barricade minor, but I took the lamp, lit it, then smashed it upon the chairs which erupted in a rush of flames.

"More," I said, and we hurried to stoke the flames. Upon our return, the parasite tested the first stair with its black limb and yanked its flopping body jarringly behind it. I could now see the Housemaid's head illuminated in unnerving blue by those spinning eerie threads. What was left of her eyes were black, and tears stained her cheeks glinting with that ethereal blue light.

I returned with more chairs, and Dr. Florence with curtains and blankets. Soon the fire roared, licked the stairs, the banister, the walls, the ornate pictures and their gaudy frames. This could have been mine, this house, if only I'd thought things through a little better. I could feel a vein in my forehead pulsing uncomfortably as I stepped back from the heat of the flames.

I turned to Dr. Florence and found her collapsed to the floor, cupping her eye. Smoke gathered around her and she coughed, then looked up at me with fear, an unnatural expression upon her stern face.

"I'll become that too," she said. "Kill me and run. Before it's too late. Kill me and run."

The orange light danced on the beads of sweat on her face, sparkling orange and gold. No, I couldn't do it. Damn the risks.

She winced, hissed, then looked at the stairs and shouted, "Willem!"

Over the banister a black outstretched tendril, extended toward me. I jumped away. "To the dining room!"

I took her by the hand and we rushed off—but before we made it, a sight caught my eye. A copper plate on the wall, behind a long, red curtain, held a series of knobs. The gas control for the lamps, for which I'd spent the previous evening searching. I let go of her hand, ran to the knobs and twisted them all open. The pipes began to hiss.

I ran back into the dining room, Dr. Florence shambling behind me and cursing the pain. She was pale and sickly, moved drunkenly, and frowned, not for self-pity—so I thought—but in a rage at the world, as if she couldn't believe she would let something as simple as her death be outside of her control.

"I don't want to burn," she seethed. "That's not how I want to die. Make it quick for me, Willem."

Oh, dear Dr. Florence. You know I could never do that. But there was something I could do, to bring her back under my control and maybe save her without a fight. Or I'd just doom the world—no way to know if I didn't try.

"I have just the thing," I said. I grabbed ether and doused a rag. Before she could protest, I grabbed her hand, pried it away, and I held the ether over her mouth until she fell limp. I looked over my shoulder to see unnatural smoke ooze into the room.

I swept much of her medical equipment into my satchel, threw the satchel over my shoulder, then lifted Dr. Florence to drag her out of the room.

An explosion sounded behind me, and the force of it threw me back a step. Smoke raked my throat and eyes. I grabbed her, yanked her back out to the landing where the creature burned and spewed a torrent of flaming gray.

I pulled Dr. Florence to the mansion's entrance as a second explosion sounded. Black smoke filled the stairway, which disappeared from view. I opened the front door, pulled Dr. Florence into the street, and slammed the door behind me.

The building burned, windows cracked then shattered, but my work wasn't done. I lay Dr. Florence on the ground, hesitating only a moment as the flames lit her face with wavering orange. Then I removed her spectacles and delved the knife into her eye.

I remember nothing of the fevered operation. When the eye was removed, I held it aloft like a trophy as the mansion spat flames sixty feet high. Then I heard the tapping of feet, was tackled to the ground and cracked in the head. Everything went white. I was dragged away by a mob who, I later learned, had seen the fire, come from their houses, then found me holding the poor doctor's eye in my bloody hands like a madman. I'm lucky they didn't kill me.

11

I spent the remainder of the night on a cold cell floor, police officers berating me as I grew ever more exhausted. Why did I kill them? Why burn down the mansion? Who was my next victim and who had I killed before now?

I remained as steely as I could, but I admit that fear ate at me. Would this be my life thenceforth? A house within prison walls, falsely accused of being a killer? It wasn't how I imagined my life would end.

They asked me why I mangled Dr. Florence, and when they saw my eyes brim with tears, they pushed harder. Again they asked, their accusations growing more insistent. Why did I disfigure her? They said she bled out on the street. Three deaths attributed to me, and as the day progressed and my stomach and heart ached, they mentioned old case files that lay dormant. It seemed I was the perfect scapegoat for every unsolved murder over the past few years.

By the evening, I was convinced that I'd hang. Their barbs no longer stung—I was numb to them. There would be a long legal process, and I'd wait and wait and wait until the day came when the noose was tied for me. I sat in the corner with my arms around my knees and tried not to think on this.

For a while, I found myself wondering what I'd done with Dr. Florence's eye. Had I thrown it in the fire? Or was it gestating somewhere, perhaps collected as evidence and sitting now within this very building, preparing to spread its foul disease? I couldn't recall, and my mind was so full of gloom, I didn't rightly care anymore.

And then I heard a commotion. The sound of protests against a stern, steady voice. I leaped to my feet. It was her! It was her! No doubt about it. She hadn't died but came for me. Her voice monotone and so forceful it made my heart pound in my chest.

The door opened, and there she was, Dr. Florence, face wrapped in gauze.

"Hello, Willem," she said.

"You came."

"Of course I did. What kind of person do you take me for? You... You saved my life, Willem." She touched the bandage gingerly, then nodded. "So I'm planning on returning the favor. How are they treating you?"

"As you'd expect," I said. "They think me a killer. It's a common theme lately, I suppose, but they seem very determined on the subject. But what of you? Your face..."

"It's fine, and I haven't displayed any symptoms. But we haven't time for that now, Willem. There is a long and arduous legal battle to be fought on your behalf. I am the only witness, and as I am a supposed victim now coming to your aid, they seem to think my judgment is questionable. I need to maintain the air of a credible witness who hasn't been influenced by you, so this will be our only meeting until this matter is resolved. My lawyers will keep you apprised of our progress over the coming weeks. Meanwhile, you'll be moving to a larger cell. I hope this situation won't be too taxing on you, but I've seen your work—I think you'll perform adequately. I hope to see you again soon, Willem."

She turned to leave, but I cried, "Wait!"

She hesitated.

"Their names," I said, tears falling from my eyes, "were Gwen and Phillip."

"Yes," she said quietly, looking at me with those... that beautiful eye.

"I just thought it important to say." I shook. I couldn't control myself for the sorrow. "I always knew, I just... I couldn't..."

"I know." She reached through the bars and placed a hand on my shoulder. "We'll get you out of here, Willem. Try not to dwell on things."

I KNOW NOT from where the strange parasite originated, but in my studies of anomalies, I have learned various hidden things about the world. This old world has many great and terrible secrets, some of which have passed with time, and others that remain dormant, waiting for the right circumstances before they rear their heads again in our world.

There are many planes which we cannot see with our eyes but, if you are special, perhaps you can sense them. That feeling in the dark when your hair stands on end. That shiver down your spine when you enter an empty room. The tickle in the back of your throat when you see floating dust catch

the light. They could be benign nothings, but in my experience, they should not be dismissed so easily.

Parasites, doppelgängers, leeches of the mind, poisons of
the soul. Always be wary. There are things more unusual than
spirits in the unseen world, creatures that survive in the
harsh environments of the aether without morals, reason, or
judgment, only an insatiable will for survival.

THE END

ACKNOWLEDGMENTS

To everyone who's supported my writing—readers, backers, editors, and friends—thank you.

Thanks especially to Tana for all of your work, your insight, and for believing in me.

And a special thank you to my patrons and beta readers for helping support the production of this book. Thanks to Radek Stepan, Brian Hague, Maria Schillaci, Melanie Ewing, Nathalie McGovern, Nick Cronquist, Rich Weston, Robert Szymanski, Scott Heron, Steven Barrus, Dave Higgins, TNae Wilcox, mrtnwild, Noelle Nichols, Joe B., Shnanign, Johnny Crow, Cesar Diaz, Joshua Crowley, J.S. Nagy, Jamie Morrison. Learn more at: https://www.patreon.com/scbarrus

THADDEUS LUMPEN & THE THEFT OF THE HOARDED MAP

AN EXCERPT FROM *DISCOVERING ABERRATION* BY S.C. BARRUS.

Lumpen and I found our seats in my study. It was a room wherein I invited few guests, Lumpen being one and Old Chap being the sole other. I always found it a bit odd when a stranger peered into this room and began quizzically looking about. Perhaps it was because the room so reflected my mind; packed with information, art, tools and years worth of useless but ornate bric-a-brac. Shelves upon shelves of frayed books, paper pamphlets, discarded leaflets, and not a few writerly manifestos which I had never found time to read but collected compulsively.

As Lumpen spoke, he nervously switched between wandering about the room while running his fingers over the spines of books and sitting anxiously, bouncing his feet as he rubbed his hands through his disheveled hair.

"You've heard of the Hammerlock Expedition, haven't you?" he scanned the room in a noncommittal manner, eyes refusing to meet mine.

"Hm," I mused. "I seem to remember it. Was that the voyage which turned to cannibalism all those years back? Lost at sea, or some other such nonsense?"

"Not quite, that was the Hamilton Expedition I believe, and they were stranded. I'm speaking of the Hammerlock Expedition. It was an exploratory voyage on behest of the Queen, God save her." He raised his flask in a sort of toast, tipped it back and frowned when he discovered it empty. "Balls'n'all. What good is the Queen if one cannot drink to her? In any event, the Hammerlock Expedition were sent south to the tropics with the mission of exploring off the shore of our southern colonies. There are a few remote islands speckled throughout that region, and I suppose the queen wanted to better understand the land around her new property."

"Ah," I pulled from my desk a bottle of brandy and poured Lumpen and myself a glass. "And what does this have to do with stealing from John-Joseph Heller of all people?"

"I'm getting to that," Lumpen retorted in a bewildered whisper, eyes wide. "And don't speak his name so loud, for heaven's sake Freddy. When you've been at the Academy as long as I have you'll learn that no good comes of even speaking an unsavory name above a whisper, and even then only when you're proper drunk and alone." He took his brandy, tipped it back with one quick swallow then returned the glass. "There are ears all about, even when you don't see them. Understand? Nobody is on each other's side these days. If the wrong person hears the wrong name, many won't think twice about reporting you to a constable. No, they can't imprison you for just saying a name, but they will take you to court and hold you until Thursday when they question you about the affair and that's bloody inconvenient, believe you me. Understand?"

"Indeed," I replied.

"Good. Now where was I?"

"The expeditions."

"Yes," he said. "The Hammerlocks. They were gone a full year longer than they had anticipated. The whole voyage was presumed a loss after it was discovered that they never made it to port at the colonies to begin with. But then, all of a sudden, they returned. Only three members of the crew remained alive and in fragile mental states. One had gone mad as a bat and couldn't speak his own name much less hold a conversation. They refused to tell of where they went or what had happened to them. Even after some... eh, questioning, no information could be extracted from them. So the survivors were brushed under the rug like an ugly secret and faded into obscurity."

"A national embarrassment," I nodded.

"Quite so, old boy. Quite so. And an expensive one. Now that was decades ago. The mad one, by the name of Murray Longbowmen, he was locked away in a chump house after questioning and, eh, died soon after. I don't know how, but I presume he either died from a result of the interrogation or he was starved or beat to death, the way those places go.

"Ten years later," he continued, "another sailor, one Phillip Smith, laid down his knife and fork, stiff as a board in a ditch outside a pub in Pristine. He was believed to have died of a substance due to the foam about his mouth, poison or drugs who knows. In any case, poor old Phillip had developed a nasty hole in his pocket, pawned everything he owned.

"And now we have the third sailor and with him a third coincidence. This one goes by the name of a Mr. Cornelius Jones."

"Dead too I expect," I presumed.

"Not quite, though he's poor as Job's turkey in body, and more recently in mind. He has become dim witted and is now dying of a blood poison. Nasty way to go really."

"Indeed." I nodded with a frown.

"Mr. Jones, the last remaining survivor of the Hammer-lock Expedition, lived in utter obscurity until just weeks ago. You see, a local journalist came across a sale at Mr. Jones's estate in Pristine and after some questioning and poking about he discovered who this man was and wrote an expose. That is how I came about learning of the unfortunate case of Cornelius Jones."

"So," I ventured, "you went to the estate sale and stole the map?"

"It's a tidy bit more complicated than that, actually. Indeed, I was quite curious so I traveled to the small estate (which was quite a small house crammed in a line with all the others on its block) to see what I could find. Of course there was also a fair share of others who had an interest in this man's story and wished to know more, including a few archeologists. A practical stampede of interested parties made the trip. But when I arrived, the sale had closed. Someone had purchased the entire estate outright, all of its assets, everything. That would have been that, as they say. Most turned back home, but Freddy, I am not most." He looked at me with a cocky raised eyebrow.

"No, Lumpen," I replied, "I dare say you are not most. You carried on."

"Ha ha! Of course I did. I couldn't simply leave and turn round like the rest of the sodding amateurs. I needed to know who had purchased the estate and why, but even more than that I needed to know if there was anything relating to the expedition within the estate. Did the buyer have any knowledge of the lost expedition?

"I could feel it in my chest," he continued. "Behind this expedition was a great and terrible secret and I wanted to be the one credited with uncovering it. I can still feel it, Freddy. So it didn't matter that searching the house, much less finding something, seemed to be far out of reach and a dangerous proposition at that.

"The buyer, whom at the time I had not a clue as to who it might be, had placed a large and ugly flat nosed guard at the entrance of Mr. Jones's house. The man stood watch at all times. He didn't even go in to piddle, if you can believe that. Simply looking at the flat nosed man put a lump in my throat, my mind begging me to turn about and run, but I've learned throughout the years to silence the inner voice. I was determined."

"That voice is called your conscience, Lumpen," I jabbed with a smile. "It may serve you to listen on occasion. Not to say I'm disappointed or would have done otherwise, but to discount your inner thought without regard?"

"Bah," he scoffed. "Conscious! We live in an amoral world, Freddy. There's no room for conscious here."

"Perhaps it is your intuition then."

"Don't lecture your elders, Freddy. I'm set in my ways and shall carry on thus."

"Elder only by ten years, you're not *that* old." I shrugged and waved a hand. "I suppose it doesn't matter. Please continue."

"Fine. The ugly brute was posted. There was no getting in during the day, that much was certain. So instead I donned a disguise, did my damnedest to remain inconspicuous, and waited. I was right to wait and ignore the voice in my head, Freddy, as you will come to realize.

"That very afternoon arrived the most modern boiler-carriage I had ever seen, a black beast of a contraption which billowed steam in great musky clouds. It was clear whoever sat within was a person of wealth and means, enough to purchase the estate and clearly more besides.

"Almost instantly," he continued, "a man in a rather uppity suit with the skin of a snake wrapped round the sleeve of his right arm emerged from the house and approached the boiler-carriage in a manner suggesting he had an entire broom lodged up his backside. A sniveling lawyer if ever I saw one. A snake is a fitting emblem for those venomous types I should think. As they spoke, I attempted to sneak ever closer, but in the end I only made out a few phrases.

"'...prepared to hand it over upon confirmation that the parties have received their payment,' said the lawyer.

"'You shall receive it tomorrow,' came a voice from the boiler-carriage so quiet it was nearly drowned in the sound of the sputtering engine, yet so authoritative it practically demanded to be heard. 'It remains untouched, the package, does it not?'

"'Of course,' said the lawyer, body rigid with anxiety though his face remained a relaxed facade.

"'Good. The house, everything inside is inconsequential.

It is only the package. Know, if it appears to have been touched I shall be... disappointed.'

"I was unable to hear much more than this other than snippets of words here and there. In any case, it was clear the lawyer was struggling to keep his wits about him. Before the boiler-carriage left, the occupant handed the lawyer a small object which fit in the palm of his hand. The lawyer didn't look at it 'til the boiler-carriage was away. With a heavy sigh of relief he blinked away the encounter and ventured to open his hand. An expression of terror washed over him and he tossed the thing aside like a hot coal, baring a scowl which suggested it was something much more sinister.

"After the lawyer returned to the house, I walked casually to where he had stood and found the thing. A screw, Freddy. A rusty, biting screw the size of a finger. It was then I knew who the man within the boiler-carriage was," Lumpen looked round the room before whispering the name, "John-Joseph Heller. There was no mistaking it." He paused in his wandering, eyes foggy as he swallowed hard and whispered, "Bloody lucky he doesn't know who has his map. Every time I think on him, a shiver creeps up my spine."

"And yet you carried on?" I questioned.

"Quite so," said Lumpen slowly, as he reached into a pocket and pulled out the screw. A dreary, nasty thing with thick, jagged threads running the length of it. This was John-Joseph Heller's other infamous trait, or alleged trait: a few times a year a body was discovered in the morning, lying in ditches near the markets or resting in an alley near the warehouses or many other such places depending on the deceased's affiliations. They were not hidden, rather they were messages. Messages bearing many half embedded screws and wide open eyes still filled with despair and pain, even in death. No one could ever pin these deaths on John-Joseph Heller beyond a reasonable doubt, but despite the lack of solid evidence, everyone knew who the culprit was. Not that it would have done much good had the authorities been certain Heller was to blame, for none knew his whereabouts.

"I did carry on," Lumpen said. "This wasn't the first time I risked my life to make a discovery. The archeological world isn't as kind as it once was, you know," Lumpen said, once again speaking with an air of confidence. "It doesn't matter who, Freddy. This is a hard won lesson for budding archeologists, but there aren't enough discoveries to go around these days and the competition isn't willing to sit back and watch you win, gain funding, get featured in the papers, and have books written about you. No, they are willing to sneak, steal, sabotage and sometimes they even kill for the sake of a discovery. John-Joseph Heller may be dangerous, but so is the archeology 102 professor next door to my office. At least Heller doesn't know who I am."

"I see," I said as I thought the matter over. Clearly Lumpen was willing to risk his life over the sake of this strange map. Would I have done the same? *Perhaps not*, thought I. *Not if it were only a map, or only a discovery. But this is not the case. This map has history, mystery, intrigue. I may not risk my life for just any archeological expedition, but for a story? For an adventure? Perhaps I would have done the same.* "Yes, I suppose I can see your point," I nodded. "So how did you end up getting the map?"

"Well," said Lumpen as he resumed pacing my study only pausing to refill his glass. "I knew from that conversation that this night would be my only chance. I would have called upon you had I the time; I suspect a few of your talents might have served to be useful. But there was no time, I was on my own. Then I got to thinking, what if what he wants had nothing to do with the Hammerlock Expedition? It didn't matter, I reasoned. There clearly was something special within the house, if not a clue about the Hammerlock Expedition, then something else clearly of value. Either way I should be able to at least turn a profit. So I waited 'til the dead of night and devised a plan.

"You see," he continued, "I had a few things to my advantage. First, the occupants had no knowledge of me so my espionage would be relatively unexpected. Second, the ugly guard seemed to be on orders not to enter the house, for the one instance he found it necessary to make a call indoors he was greeted with a wealth of harsh words from the lawyer. And third, there appeared to only be three of them: the guard, the lawyer and the dying old man. I am a gambling man, Freddy, and I liked those odds.

"Night came and I scouted the premises. I reasoned it might be best to approach from the rear rather than risk being caught by the guard. This was a townhouse, one of many squashed all mish-mashed in a dense line as I said before, so to do this I was forced to walk to the end of the block and sneak through the narrow back alley.

"Through the dark alley I crept under glowing windows which cast squares of lamp light upon the ground. As I neared what I assumed to be the correct house, I realized I hadn't counted how many townhomes were between Mr. Jones's house and the end of the line. I panicked. They all looked the same from the back, all gray with the same patterned windows and nondescript style. I settled my nerves and inferred I was at the correct home. My heart in my throat, I approached a darkened window and to my dismay found it barred.

"'Curse my wretched luck,' I hissed. Scowling, nearly blind in the dark, I looked for some way I could infiltrate but when my probing found nothing, I realized that combat might be my only option."

"Combat?" I said with a laugh of surprise. "With one of John-Joseph Heller's cronies?"

"Quite. I can fight, Freddy," he frowned. "Remember that pub on Bakers Street? I gave that mathematics professor arsehole a fine beating, you remember don't you?"

"I remember you getting hit in the head with a bottle and losing your timber. You were out cold, Lumpen."

"Never mind that, I was winning up until that point anyway. Cheating with a bottle, of all the bloody things. Next time Freddy, no mistake he'll see how it goes when one faces off with an archeologist."

"But you didn't fight the guard, did you?" I asked. "Clearly you are still standing."

"No," he said annoyed. "As it turns out combat wasn't entirely necessary, not in the strictest sense anyway. And thus we see how ignoring my inner voice paid off a second time. I knew this argument would come back round in my favor. Now, where was I? Let us save the questions for the end, you keep pulling me out of my rhythm."

"You avoided combat."

"Ah, yes," Lumpen said with a finger in the air. "With the guard at any rate. I was furious as I made my way back. I was so angry I kicked a ladder which lay along the ground, then cursed the damned thing for stubbing my toe. I had nearly left the alley, fists gripped tight as I prepared my mind for a bout, but then I realized: the ladder! It would be the very object I exercised my anger against that would grant me access!

"I grabbed the ladder and carried the heavy thing down the way 'til I reached the home I supposed was correct. It took a good deal of work to lift it and prop it up against the roof without making too much of a racket, but I just managed and worked my way up the first story, then the second 'til I reached the rooftops.

"I'm not fond of heights," he said, "so I was damn sure glad to be off of that warbling ladder and on solid footing again. As I supposed, there was a way in, a small door leading into the attic, and from the dusty attic into the dark second floor. All that remained was to have a look about and find whatever there was to discover.

"Nervously I crept from room to room peering in as I passed, all the while on lookout for the bed ridden old man. I've never broken into a stranger's house before, so I was not keen on idling any longer than absolutely necessary. The most likely place something valuable was hidden, I thought to myself, was in reach of the old bugger, Mr. Cornelius Jones. But the rooms of the top floor were dark and without occupants. Searching each room quietly, I pocketed a thing or two as a sort of insurance against not finding anything at all, but when all the top rooms had been searched, nothing of note had turned up other than a little silver.

"I had especially hoped to avoid the lower floor if at all possible but it seemed I had no other choice if I truly wanted to etch my name in the history books. That is the difference between great men and small, we great are willing to do the hard things, the uncomfortable things to ensure we succeed. With stalwart conviction, I tip toed down the stairs. With knightly bravery, I darted from shadow to shadow. But it was just my luck, as I took up hiding next to a cabinet, the damn thing shook with a clatter. A voice issued from down the hall.

"'Did you hear something, Cassandra?' came the voice of an older man.

"I stood on edge as if lightning had just struck my spine. This was not the correct house! It couldn't be. The things in my pockets were not that of Cornelius Jones nor soon to be John-Joseph Heller's.

"Footsteps rounded the corner and I fumbled about looking for a means to my escape. Should I dash out the front door and surely be seen by the ugly guard, giving away any chance I might have to fix this error? Should I show this poor occupant a fight and give him what-for just to carry out this robbery? He hadn't seen me proper when a thought struck me. The correct house was likely only one over, after all I had been rather careful in my guessing.

"'Time to get inventive, eh,' I told myself as I prepared for another gamble. East or west? Fifty, fifty chance. I chose east and began to sneak in that direction when my hair stood on end as the old man shouted, 'Cassandra, fetch me musket. Quickly does it, I think we've got a burglar.'

"Panic pressed against my chest with sudden pressure. I could hardly breathe as the thought of my life coming to a sudden end here in this old man's house took hold of my mind. Time was short, death on my coattails. Heart thumping in my ears, I shot toward the next room, the kitchen, and frantically searched for something to make use of before a lead ball made its acquaintance with my arse. And there it was clear as day, my savior in good times and in bad, the object of my affection to which I owe my very life. Gin.

"I made a lunge for the counter and grabbed the two full bottles in either sweaty hand. From down the hall came the cautious footsteps of the man. 'I know you're in there,' he called as he approached. 'I can hear you mucking about you addled bastard. You on something? You fiending for opium are you? I've got your opium right here.'

"At the kitchen doorway, I quickly peeked round the corner. In that instant, all I saw was the man standing square in the center of the hall, then a sudden flash as the gun roared, the bullet flew and behind me the door-frame exploded into a shower of splinters.

"This was my chance. It was the old style musket which is just about all you see amongst common folk, as he hurried to re-load I burst back into the hall. Running toward the cast wall, I lifted one bottle in the air and chucked it against the wall where it shattered into diamond shards and alcohol. I raised the second bottle when the man shouted, 'I may be old, but I'm as quick as any devil with a musket. Hold still you... you vagabond!'

"I stood shaking, swallowing down my fear, clenching my jaw and forcing myself into a state of fury. When the gun did not fire, I peered over my shoulder where I saw the old man in night gown and cap shacking fiercely as he held his musket.

"'Whomever you may be,' cried the old man, 'if you value your life you'll drop that bottle where you stand.'

"'Drop the bottle?' I questioned.

"'Aye,' the man ordered, 'Drop it.'

"'That's the whole idea,' I said. With a powerful throw, the second bottle plummeted toward the wall where it burst. I ducked to my knees quickly and pulled a match from my pocket when I heard a second *crack!* from the musket. The wall before me spit a small plumb of debris only inches from my head. I struck the match and held it against the wall. It took to flame brilliantly and spread along the wall and floor like the gates of hell.

"The man cried out and his wife screamed behind him as the wall burned fiercely. There I was standing before it like a nightmare. I waited for a moment as Cassandra dashed for water and the man fumbled with fear and anger, staring me down with venom in his eyes.

"Though the wall burned hot it required more time before my plan could come to fruition. Turning on the old man, I eyed him in my most menacing way. 'I have no quarrel with you,' I shouted, 'and I am only within your house by way of a bad mistake, but I will not abide by being shot and will disarm you if you force me. Soon the wall will be in cinders and then your house with it. I will not stop you from gathering water with your wife, nor will I stop you from calling on the fire brigade, but don't you try and stop me or I'll show you what it's like.'

"Of course this was all acting. I had not a gun on my person nor a weapon of any kind other than the old man's silverware I had pocketed. Even so, the man quivered. He may have been experienced once, but time had worn away his fighting spirit. His eyes on the roaring flame, he dropped the gun and ran to meet his wife to gather water.

"Turning back to the wall, the fire had spread, licking the ceiling as it burned the wall black. This is what I had been waiting for. I backed away by seven or eight paces and eyed it warily. 'Have I done anything more ridiculous than this I wonder?' I asked myself as the wall glowed hot and dangerous. 'Anything for the discovery,' I reasoned. 'Anything for recognition after all these years.'

"I nearly charged when from the corner of my eye a chair caught my attention. 'Ah,' I thought, 'that'll do.' I grabbed the chair, hoisted it up and hammered it against the burning wall. Swinging once, then again, the chair burst through one side as sparks and ash filled the air. Then I tossed the chair to the side and stepped back.

"I rushed the wall like I was an evil knight on horseback and when I was near the flames, I covered my face with my arms and plowed forward shoulder at the fore. I met the wall in a burst of blunt force, pain, and fiery fury. The wall gave way and in a second I was tripping through the rough hole, falling triumphantly burnt and bruised on the other side.

"When I looked up from the ash and debris, there stood the lawyer looking dumbfounded. Slowly I rose to my feet and beat the dust from my jacket. The lawyer slowly backed away, first one step, then another. I tilted my head as I eyed him dangerously. At this he spun round and cried, 'Burk! Burk, get in here quick damn you.'

"Round the corner came the voice of the guard, 'So now it's awlright then? Now I can come in? Ya sure? Ya sure you want me ta muck up them nice carpets?'

"But before the lawyer had time to answer I was middash, bearing on him quickly. I leaped upon the man and the two of us crashed to the ground. The poor bugger began to slap at me, which was more annoying than dangerous. It didn't take much to get him in a head lock and whisper in his ear, 'Alright pansy, my partner's already got everything. He'll be coming out of the room momentarily.' Of course this was a lie, I had no partner, but I did study psychology while a student at the academy. I watched the poor bastard's eyes and they flickered in the direction of a door at the end of the hall. That was my clue, whatever it was John-Joseph Heller was after was certainly in that room.

"'Is efryfing awlright in there?' The ugly guard called in from the doorway. Smoke was already filling the room and the couple in the other town home were making a racket as they gathered bowls of water and tossed them upon the flames.

"I had no more time. Everything hinged on how I handled this moment. I tightened my grip on the lawyers neck, flexing and pulling against his neck until his head went limp. A technique practiced on brothers growing up, this was quite easy. I jumped to my feet as the guard rounded the corner.

"'There's been a horrific accident in my grandfather's house. A fire. We need help putting the wretched thing out or everything we own will burn into dust. Quick now, quick, fetch some water. Have you any elderly in here, you best point me in their direction, if this man has already fainted from the fumes I can only imagine how hard it will be on frailer souls.'

"He watched the chaos in silence, piecing together the scene bit by bit in his mind.

"'Quick man, quick,' I shouted. 'At the very least you can run grab the fire brigade! Go before you lose everything too.'

"'Aye,' he said as his face twisted in frustration. 'Shite, the boss is gonna piss 'imself when he hears of this.' He turned and ran out the door.

"Behind me the fire burned in full force as the elderly couple put one final hard lost effort. Before me was everything I needed, Freddy. Everything. My mind focused on that singular thought as I raced down the hall to the door and burst through. There slept Mr. Jones, his breath wheezing, and smelling to high heaven of a putrid mixture of smoke and elixirs.

"Frantically, I raced about the room looking over dressers, within cabinets, about the floor. I threw items to the side angrily as I searched. Peeking back, the lawyer was slowly gaining consciousness, panic stricken as he turned round to witness the breadth of the flames. 'Think,' I demanded of myself, 'Think damn it! Where would an old man hide something so valuable? He would keep it close, keep it out of sight, but somewhere he could check on it.'

"And then it hit me. I dropped to my hands and knees and scurried to the side of his bed, my head getting dizzy with the smoke and the pungent, stinging smell of ammonia, iodine, and laxatives. An ancient, wrinkled arm hung off the side of the bed like the hand of death, veins blue, skin like paper. A finger hung as if pointing to my destiny and I drew closer. When I peered beneath the bed, there I found an old wooden box locked shut. As I pulled it out the old Mr. Jones, hardly aware of life itself, reached out for it, fingers brushing the lid but unable to grasp it. I had no time to open it, but when I saw the seal of the Queen branded upon the wood, I knew. 'This is it,' I said to myself, 'a relic from that long ago journey, it must be.'

"So I held it under my arm and ran for my life."

READ DISCOVERING ABERRATION

When Freddy was young, he was enmeshed in the underground world of illegal street fighting. As a teacher, his sedate life leaves him thirsting for adventure.

When his friend, Lumpen, confesses to have stolen an ancient map from a crime lord, they join forces to unearth the discovery of a lifetime.

They'll set halfway around the world in a race against the criminal underworld and vindictive rivals. They may expect violence, but they'll discover madness.

Read Discovering Aberration today, only on Amazon.

FIND S.C. BARRUS ONLINE

Blog - awayandaway.com

Newsletter - awayandaway.com/newsletter

Patreon - www.patreon.com/scbarrus

Goodreads - www.goodreads.com/scbarrus

Twitter - twitter.com/scbarrus

Instagram - instagram.com/authorscbarrus

www.ingramcontent.com/pod-product-compliance
Lightning Source LLC
Chambersburg PA
CBHW030607130626
46552CB00006B/2684